Mr. Pine's Mixed-up Signs

BOOKS STARRING MR. PINE

Mr. Pine's Mixed-up Signs

Mr. Pine's Purple House

Mrs. Pine Takes a Trip

Paint Me a Picture, Mr. Pine

Mr. Pine's Storybook

Mr. Pine's Mixed-up Signs

Story and Pictures by
LEONARD KESSLER

Editorial Consultant
LILIAN MOORE

Purple House Press
Kentucky

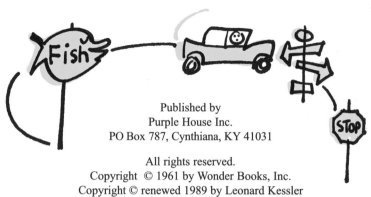

Published by
Purple House Inc.
PO Box 787, Cynthiana, KY 41031

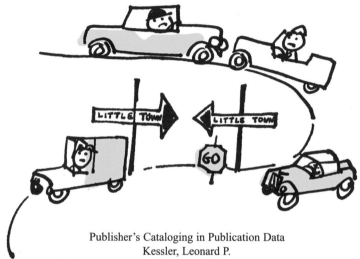

Publisher's Cataloging in Publication Data
Kessler, Leonard P.
Mr. Pine's mixed-up signs / story and pictures by Leonard Kessler;
[edited by] Lilian Moore p. cm.
SUMMARY: Mr. Pine paints all new signs for Little Town then loses his glasses, creating chaos after the signs become mixed up.
[1. Signs — Fiction. 2. People — Fiction. 3. Towns — Fiction.] I. Moore, Lilian. II. Title.
PZ7.K484 Mi 2001   [E] - dc21 2001091391
ISBN-13: 978-1-930900-03-5

www.PurpleHousePress.com

Printed in South Korea by PACOM
3 4 5 6 7 8 9 10

When I was a young child, I was fascinated with signs. . . all kinds of signs.

Mike, our next door neighbor, was an artist and sign painter. His sign shop was in the front room of his house.

I would sit and watch him paint those wonderful signs.

"Lenny," he would say, "I am not just painting signs, but I am helping people. I am giving them information. Look." He held up a sign. . . a STOP sign.

"It is very important for drivers to stop their cars at this sign. Stop signs can save lives," he said.

Mike showed me more signs. "This is one of my favorites," he said.

ICE CREAM CONES. 5¢ one scoop.

10¢ two scoops.

These are some of the first words I learned to read:

ONE WAY • PETS • BARBER • GAS • TOYS
FISH • BANK • BAKERY • SHOES

Readers often ask, "Where do you get ideas for your books?"

Sometimes from a child's question, "Are we lost Daddy?" Sometimes from one of my five senses, sometimes from my imagination, and sometimes from events that I remember. . . such as those early happy days in Mike's sign shop.

INTRODUCTION

These books are meant to help the young reader discover what a delightful experience reading can be. The stories are such fun that they urge the child to try new reading skills. They are so easy to read that they will encourage and strengthen the child as a reader.

The adult will notice that the sentences aren't too long, the words aren't too hard, and the skillful repetition is like a helping hand. What the child will feel is: "This is a good story — and I can read it myself!"

For some children, the best way to meet these stories may be to hear them read aloud at first. Others, who are better prepared to read on their own, may need a little help in the beginning — help that is best given freely. Youngsters who have more experience in reading alone — whether in first or second grade — will have the immediate joy of reading "all by myself."

These books have been planned to help all young readers grow — in their pleasure in books and in their power to read them.

Lilian Moore
Specialist in Reading
Formerly of Division of Instructional Research,
New York City Board of Education

Mr. Pine made signs.

He made signs that said

He made signs that said

He made signs that said

And signs that said

9

Mr. Pine made all the signs
in Little Town.
A town needs many signs.
It needs signs for roads. . .
and streets
and stores.

Mr. Pine made them all
for Little Town.

He painted big signs.

He painted little signs.

He painted signs with words.

He painted signs with pictures.

"Go this way."

"Go that way."

Or signs that said:

"Look out—a road will cross."

"Slow down! Hole in the road!"

Yes, Little Town
had all the signs
a town could need.

But, little by little, the signs
in Little Town
got old.
The rain and the snow
fell on the signs.

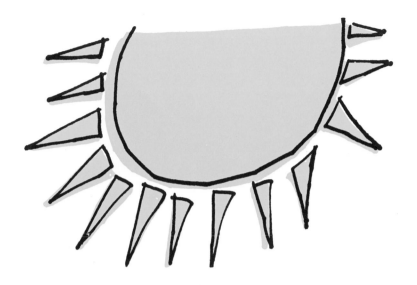

The wind blew them
and the hot sun baked them.

Soon no one
could tell
what the signs said.

"We need new signs,"
said the Mayor of Little Town.
"I will go to see Mr. Pine."
And he did.

"Mr. Pine, we need new signs
all
over
Little
Town,"
said the Mayor.
"Will you make them for us?"

"Oh, yes, yes," said Mr. Pine.

"I like to make signs.

I will paint them all

and I will put them up, too."

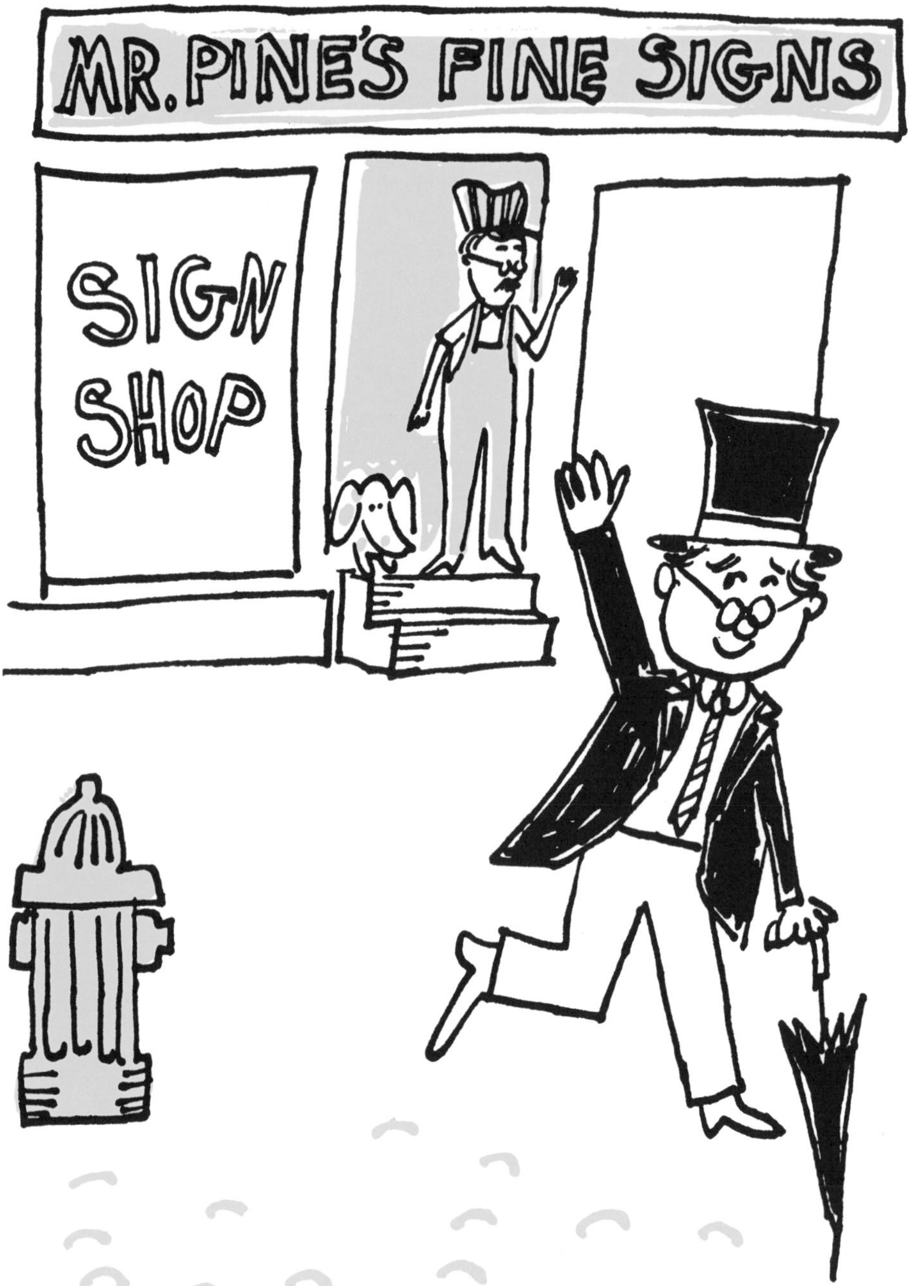
MR. PINE'S FINE SIGNS
SIGN SHOP

"We need them
right away," said the Mayor.
"I will do them
right away," said Mr. Pine.
"You will have them all
in one week!"

23

The next week Mr. Pine

painted and painted

and painted.

He painted big signs.

He painted little signs.

He painted round signs.

He painted red signs

and blue signs and green signs.

At the end of the week

all the new signs were done.

"Now I must let the signs dry,"
said Mr. Pine.
"Then I can put them up
in the morning."

In the morning Mr. Pine

got out of bed.

"Where are my glasses?"

Mr. Pine said.

27

He looked here:

and here:

and here:

and even HERE!

He looked everywhere.
But did not see
his glasses.
"Where can they be?"
he said.
"Oh, dear, everything
looks so funny!
I wish I had my glasses."

Everything did look
funny.
But Mr. Pine had
to put up the signs.
So out he went.

Soon the new signs were up
all over Little Town.
Mr. Pine did not know it,
but the signs looked funny, too!

The town looked like this:

and like this:

and like THIS!

Did you ever see a town look
like this?

Mr. Jones, the baker, went
to open his store.
The sign over the door
of his store said
"HATS FOR SALE"

Mr. Clark went to open
his shoe store.
The sign on the window
said "GAS 33¢"

Mr. Hill went to open
his candy store.
The sign
on the door
said
"PET SHOP
Cats and Dogs
for Sale"

Mrs. Brown went
to open her bookstore.
What did she see?
A big sign
that said
"NO PARKING
AT ANY TIME"

Every sign on every store

on every street

on every road

was new,

but

they were

all

MIXED UP.

Over the bank

the sign said

"BREAD"

The sign on Main Street
said
"Candy 5¢"
And the sign
on the Mayor's door
said
"THIS WAY
TO THE
ZOO"

"Find Mr. Pine!"
cried the Mayor.
"Find him fast!"

Soon everyone was looking
for Mr. Pine.
Where was Mr. Pine?

He was looking

for his glasses.

"Where can they be?" he said

again and again.

The cars in Little Town
were going round
and round.
Everyone was
all mixed up.

One sign

said Stop.

One sign

said Go.

One sign

said Fast.

One sign

said Slow.

Stop. Go.

Fast. Slow.

—all mixed up!

"Find Mr. Pine!"
cried the Police Officer.

And where was Mr. Pine?

Mr. Pine was still looking

for his glasses.

"Did I put them here?

Or did I put them here?" he said.

"I must find
my glasses. I want
to see all my fine
new signs."

He looked everywhere.
At last he looked here:

And there they were!
How happy Mr. Pine was
to have found
his glasses!
He ran to the window
and looked out.
"Oh, no!" he said.
"Oh, no!"

He saw this:

"Oh! Oh!" cried Mr. Pine.

"What a mix-up!"

He ran to find

the Mayor.

The Mayor

was running

to find him.

"Mr. Pine," said the Mayor.

"Mr. Mayor,"

said Mr. Pine.

Then together they cried,

"The signs are

all mixed up!"

"I will fix them
right away,"
said Mr. Pine.
And he did.

Soon the new signs
were in the right
place.
Soon Little Town looked
all right again.
But no one will ever forget
Mr. Pine and the mixed-up signs!

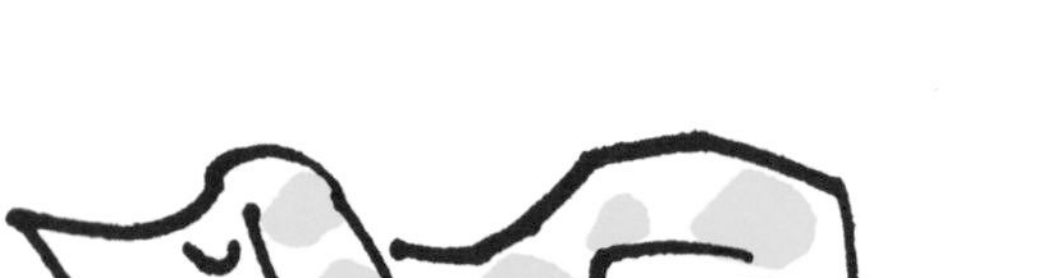